Love Isn't Always
On Time

Tiffany Forbes

DEDICATION

To my loves Ke'Shayla and Jaylah

LOVE ISN'T ALWAYS ON TIME

CHAPTER 1 ZAYVION

Everywhere I go there is a woman trying to get my attention and today was no different. From church to the grocery store, there is always an overzealous female who seems just a little too friendly or is just outright bold. Impatiently waiting for my change and my receipt I stand in line at my favorite store, Walmart. The bold female licks her lips spreading the silver colored matte lipstick across her lips looking as if she just ate her fair share of powdered donuts. To top that off she had thick black liner outlining her lips. For that reason alone, I could not take her seriously. The cashier, whose name was Moni, scribbled something down on the receipt so fast it was almost illegible. Pressing the change and the short strip of paper in my hand she winked, batting her long faux eyelashes. I guess that was an attempt at a seductive sexy gesture.

Hell, I don't know but I was tired. I stopped by the store after work to pick up some bottled water laundry detergent, and a few snacks. I had been at work for over twelve hours and once I got home I had no plans of coming back out tonight.

Smiling she showed her one gold tooth in the front when she spoke, "Zay, baby you need to stop playing and hit me up sometimes. Shit, I get off in five minutes. I can get you off. What's up?" She put the last item in the bag with my snacks, coming around the register to place my bag in the cart. I guess she wanted to show off that big beach ball booty behind her. She certainly did have an ass. I smiled because I liked the view. It was nothing wrong with looking but she was off the chain getting straight to the point like that, I had no words for that. I was always told if you don't have anything nice to say then don't say anything so I just kept quiet.

She eyed me all over like a piece of meat the way a lion does its prey. If I was down for asking her to roll with me I'm sure she would have made time to play right now. I guess she was waiting for a response. I was not about that life. I was faithful and dedicated to my girl.

Standing at over six feet, 6'5 will dark chocolate skin, the ladies love me. I play basketball and go to hit the gym up in my free time so my body is nice. I won't say I'm the most muscular brother around but I'm not slacking either. I spend long days walking a lot at the warehouse where I work at as supervisor. Damn near all day long, twelve hour shifts five or six days a week I'm active and on the move. So yeah I had a nice body. Never cocky or conceited I know I'm a handsome guy so I was used to shit like this now.

"Moni, a brother is tired and I need to be getting home."

I was trying to avoid being rude and here she was smiling like she won the lottery. I didn't need her getting all confrontational and crazy causing a scene because I turned her down. Looking at the high yellow blonde cashier standing across from me she wasn't ugly and she just wasn't my type. I was taken and that was all that mattered.

She knew this because I came in this store daily often with

3

my family, she just didn't give a damn.

"Make sure you use that number baby. I know what a fine man like you needs after working all day!" She cackled as I walked away pretending not to hear her.

After putting my items in the backseat I looked at the address and phone number I saw that she didn't live too far from me. As soon as I pulled out of the parking lot I threw the number out the window. I was completely faithful to my fiancé Jonelle Todd; I didn't have any use for it.

Zayvion Black is my name. I'm a twenty-four-year-old father and fiancé. Right now my ambition and goals kept me going; I had a family to feed and they were depending on me. I was working hard because I had goals to buy my girl and daughter a house before we got married in a year. Not the least bit interested in another woman I had everything I wanted right at home. I couldn't wait to get home to see the light in my life Jonelle. We were years in our relationship and had the type of relationship that most people wanted. If things would have been different Jonelle would have had my daughter after she had my last name but I loved her and I was going to make her

Mrs. Black so it didn't matter. She was all that I needed in life.

I've had my share of women from dark skin to light skin, from black to white, thick to thin but no woman can compare to my baby Jonelle. Jonelle is a slim brown skin bombshell with a cute button nose, full lips, and big almond eyes, her skin is the color of rich hot cocoa. Her looks have always captivated me. She had model qualities and she knew it. Just thinking about her made me smile and I couldn't wait to get home to my beautiful girl.

In no time I had made it to our luxury apartment. I couldn't wait to see my baby after being away from home all day.

Balancing the stuff in my arms I opened the door.

My smile had quickly turned upside down as called out, "Jonelle!"

Not playing any games, I brought the thirty-six pack of bottled water and two shopping bags in with one trip. I was not going back out to the car making a second trip. I set everything down on the counter before I dropped anything. Walking into the kitchen of our spacious loft style three-bedroom apartment Jonelle was nowhere to be found.

Dishes were piled up in the sink and garbage overflowed out the trash can. How could one person make such a mess in twelve hours?

The place was spotless when I left because I cleaned up last night while Jonelle sat on the plush oversized sofa with a facial mask on, with flexi rollers in her long hair that cost me damn near a check, with that barking ass little dog beside her watching Love and Hip Hop, completely ignoring me. She sipped on a tall glass of ice water with lemons, with all her undivided attention on her show.

Last Night

"Move back Zay. I can't see with you in front of the tv. You're going to make me miss the good part." Jonelle spoke with her deep raspy voice.

I moved out the way. A brother couldn't even get a hug or hello. She was like that when her shows came on. The way she carried on she should have been on a reality show. Right now my reality sucked.

I was tired horny and hungry after a long day of work. Instead of having her man some dinner done and bath water ran she was in here in a tank and boy shorts chilling like she was right. I busted my ass to make sure she didn't have to work so I wasn't asking Jonelle for much. All day long while I worked I don't know what the hell she did.

Looking around the kitchen it definitely wasn't cleaning.

"Well hello to you too, Jonelle. My day went ok."

I was being sarcastic since she didn't even take the time to speak. With my deep voice I spoke in a smooth mellow tone, I know she heard me yet my greeting fell on deaf ears. To avoid cussing her out or being childish like her, I headed to the bathroom in our room to take a shower. In the past when our love was new and endless she would have melted at the sound of my voice like butter on a hot summer day.

She would have greeted me at the door with something sexy on. She would have had the house spotless and my food would have been hot and ready. Jonelle would've even joined me in the shower to help wash away the funk of the day. I used to be able to count on her to lovingly wash my back and I do the same to her, easing all my stress and tensions of the long days away. I would run my fingers through her hair as the shower water cascaded upon us. Her large sweet lips would taste so sweet as I savored them in the shower. Grabbing her neck sensually I would press her body against the shower wall and place her leg on the shower bench getting behind her just the way she loved it as the water beat off our bodies as I beat it up. Many nights I would make passionate sweet love to her after work right here bathing in her love and essence.

Times had really changed.

There would be no romantic moments stolen under the water tonight. Lathering my thick manhood, I couldn't help but rise to attention as I thought about the memories that seemed to be tucked away. Deciding against self-gratification I quickly I scrubbed my body off because I had to make me something to eat. I worked through lunch today trying to make sure that my staff made production and now I was hungry.

Dinner would not fix itself. All showered and fresh thirty minutes later I felt like a new man. The shower had relaxed me a bit. After slipping on some basketball shorts I went into the kitchen.

My manhood was free as I walked. I wanted to taunt her a

little. I knew how to make her all hot and bothered. I stood in front of her so she could see the outline of what I was working with. Jonelle looked up at me as she polished her toes and had her phone resting on her shoulder up to her ears. She licked her lips. Before the night was over I wanted her sweet candy coated kisses all over me.

Her little Pomeranian laid on her side as she continued to pamper herself. That damn dog got more attention than me. Maybe tonight I would get lucky, though. Over the past few weeks, she always had an excuse not to give me no poom poom and when she did follow through with her wifely duties she made it the laziest sex and took the fun out of it. She acted like she was the one working twelve hour shifts.

Making my way into the kitchen, I didn't have time to dwell on any of that right now as my stomach was touching my back. I reached down in the cabinet and pulled out a frying pan so I could fry some chicken wings, never taking my eyes of Jonelle as I waited on the grease to heat up. I wanted to talk to her but she was still on the phone talking to one of her girls. I didn't want to start an argument with her because her giving me

9

some loving was definitely would definitely be out the window then.

Instead, I rinsed the sink full of dishes and loaded the black dishwasher that complemented the all black appliances in the kitchen. Next, I pulled out some frozen corn on the cob to go with my chicken. I could cook better than my girl believe it or not. She loved for me to cook for her, I had spoiled her.

As my food cooked I cleaned up in the kitchen. I couldn't stand a dirty house. The kitchen was a wide open space, an L-shaped center island with black granite countertop and deep black double sinks divided the living room and kitchen. One end there were tall black chairs, on the other side was a bar that sheltered my top shelf alcohol. It was perfect for entertaining guest. The picturesque living room was spacious with hardwood floors and a wall mounted flat tv that spread the span of the room. The high ceiling and exposed wood beams made the room seem very large. Speakers were strategically placed so the surround sound would fill the room. In the living room area, large windows showed off the natural beauty of the surrounding landscape of the Appomattox River, not too far from Virginia State University, where the lofts were located.

The oversized burgundy chairs with the black accent tables went perfectly with the large black and white family pictures splashed with burgundy hung on the brick walls. The adjacent walls were white with black crown molding. My favorite photo of them all was the photo of me, Jonelle and Joy when she was about a year old that sat above the fireplace, which was a focal point in our home. It was the same striking black marble as the nearby bar, wall-sized fireplace often showcased a mesmerizing row of flames that would often bring warmth to the space. The mantel lends itself well to holiday décor during the holidays, while the crackling fire and warmth of my beloved used to provide the best excuse to stay home on a Saturday night. Recently I spent many Saturday nights alone.

Staring at the picture, Jonelle looked so happy back then. I wish I could get those days back. If she wasn't happy neither was I. The old saying a happy wife equals a happy life. I was miserable when she got in her ways.

Looking around our home I must say she did one hell of a job decorating the place. That too was a happy time for

Jonelle, when she was playing interior decorator. Adjacent to the kitchen was a short hallway that led to the smallest bedroom that we used as a guest bedroom and the other bathroom. The only guest who seemed to stay were her friends who never could seem to make it home.

On the left side of the living room and kitchen were the two other much larger bedrooms, one which we shared and the other one belonging to Joy decorated in a pink princess theme and lots of toys. The closets were full of unworn clothes for Jonelle and Joy with tags still on them.

The more money I made the more she spent, too bad she didn't give a damn about keeping our home spotless now. She was always on the go. The question that always lingered in my mind was what did she do all damn day?

She shopped and talked on her phone and sometimes she babysat our daughter Joy. Yes, I said babysit. She would watch our child from time to time because her mother had her majority of the time. To be a stay at home mother Jonelle never had our child with her. Her mother watched Joy most of the time because I worked long hours while Jonelle claimed she needed a break.

The delicious smell of hot fried chicken, with buttered corn on the cob and biscuits, invited her into the kitchen as she pulled up a seat smiling showing her neat teeth. Her mother had invested a lot of money and time with the dental work on her. She was a spoiled only child and she brought that idea into the relationship.

"I'm glad that you cooked dinner, Zay. I thought I was going to have to order something to eat."

Jonelle had a deep voice to be a woman. Her voice paired with her diva attitude, it fit her persona perfectly. With her tall height and slim body, she could have been a model. Anything she wanted I would have supported her to the fullest. Unfortunately, she didn't want too much but be seen and stunt on her imaginary haters, clubbing and partying. I bet she spent the day posting simple shit online when she should have been doing something productive. She should have cooked and cleaned to start.

Here she was now pulling up a seat at the bar after I cooked. I had the thought not to cook her anything to eat because it was going on almost ten at night and she sat around hungry waiting on me to cook. Shit was out of hand.

"It wouldn't have hurt you to cook dinner Jonelle."

"Well, I did take the chicken out for you. I figured you would want something to eat when you got off work."

I just looked at her and begin to eat my food. Chewing my food slowly I enjoyed the quick meal I put together. I'm really glad my mother taught me how to cook and clean. She liked to pretend she didn't hear me a lot of times so right now I was just paying her back. Ignorance didn't deserve a response.

Looking into her big eyes I studied her hoping to see how or why did we get to this point.

She was so busy devouring her food like it was the last supper. Her wings didn't stand a chance after she drowned them in hot sauce and broke her biscuits up covering them with butter. She had already eaten two ears of corn. Just because she was model thin did not mean she ate light like a model. Trying to lighten the mood because regardless of how she annoyed me or irritated me, I could not stay angry or upset with her.

I put my dishes in the sink and stood behind Jonelle, kissing her neck as she sat on the tall chair. Surprisingly she pushed her plate away and turned to face me. She begins to lock lips with me in a passionate, sensual kiss.

With her tongue down my throat, she was making my man come to life. Dinner was satisfying so but I still had a taste for something sweet. I wanted some of those sweet candied yams between her thighs for my desert. I could not get enough of her sweetness. She would be my desert.

Before I knew it, I had stepped out of my shorts, finally free releasing myself. Her eyes danced in amazement. I hope that she was ready for me. Standing up she stood almost the same height as me. No words needed to be spoken as she pulled off her boy shorts exposing her shaved fat cat, looking me in the eyes. Smelling sweet and fragrant like sweet juicy peaches I had to have this girl right now. I stroked my thickness, it was a handful or in her case two. When she held me she would always need two hands as she pleased me.

Sitting her small ass that she loves to think was voluptuous on the cold counter she pulled off her shirt allowing her pretty mocha colored girls to spring free. My mouth watered in anticipation as to what was about to come. I could taste it as I salivated. Looking between her center she was dripping wet. Her juices leaked on the counter top. Moving closer I dove in for my sweet desert, licking her up and down as she begged for it. She satisfied my craving and I made sure that she was pleased. From the kitchen, living room to the bedroom I gave Jonelle everything that she needed.

I loved her down all through the house. Finally tired we both crawled into bed and feel asleep in each other's arms the way we would do in the past. If I could only get more nights like this than we would be okay. Sleep never felt so good, especially with the girl of your dreams nestled beside you laying on your chest. As much as I wanted to lay right here and hold my baby morning came quickly.

Sunlight came beaming through the blinds. It was time for me to get up and make another day. Reaching over for Jonelle she was no longer beside me. I could smell the aroma of bacon. Throwing the comforter back I rolled out of bed with a big smile to take care of my morning duties before showering.

Baby girl had already showered too, the fragrance of her body wash and perfume lingered in the bathroom air. This was too good to be true. I put that thing on her last night for her to be up early cooking breakfast and showered this early. Normally she slept late. She didn't even get up to get Joy ready for in the morning because I dropped her off at daycare. I felt like the man this morning. Nothing or nobody could ruin my day today.

After dressing I brushed my low cut and looked at my appearance. Pleased with my appearance I made my way to the table where my plate of bacon, eggs, cheese, bagels, juice, and coffee awaited me. Jonelle sat at the table with her long hair down, the curls falling perfectly in place wearing jeans and button up shirt. Her makeup was on point too as I noticed the lipstick covering her luscious lips.

I noticed her favorite pair of red bottom heels by the couch when I walked in the room. Where was she going this early?

Getting up to kiss me I found that odd because normally when she put on her makeup and beat her face as she loved to call it she didn't like to kiss me for fear of me ruining her makeup. This morning she gently pressed her lips to mine and gave me the best kiss. What a way to wake your man up. She was on one today and I was loving it.

"Good morning baby." Her deep voice made you think she could sing.

"Morning Jonelle. Thanks for the breakfast." I dug in and ate my food. As much as I would have loved to chop it up I had a thirty-five to forty-five-minute drive to work depending on traffic.

"You're welcome."

"I'm sorry Zayvion. I just wanted to apologize for my attitude lately."

"I love you Jonelle. I have loved you since high school and all relationships go through things. I'm never going to give up on you or us."

I should have known she was being sweet and apologetic for a reason.

Biting down on her lip, she gave me the fake shy look. "Zay, I need five hundred dollars."

Being the good man that I am, I didn't even ask her why. I'm sure it was for a good reason. I went into my wallet and handed her four one hundred dollar bills that was all the cash that I had on me at the time. After the way she performed last night my wife could have every dime I had. And I didn't want to be late for work so I gave her what I had. If I so happened to need anything I could use my debit card or just go to the ATM.

"Here you go. Thanks for the breakfast. And thanks for last night. I love you. I'll see you when I get off work. Maybe we can do something."

Jonelle put the bills in her purse and reluctantly said "Sure. We can do something.".

We kissed again before I had to leave for work. I saw myself to my car as she locked the door behind me.

Hitting the unlock button I got in and turned on the music. I drove a black Lexus with rims. It was the same car that I had for the last three years. I wanted to get a new car but I drove the same one so Jonelle could have the BMW she drove. For her birthday a few months ago I had gone all out, getting her the car she wanted. I surprised her with a dark blue five series with a big red bow on it. She dropped hints that she wanted the car so I busted my ass to get it for her. Her car was nicer and newer than what I drove. As long as I got from point a to point be I was not complaining but she had to have all the newest shit. After finding some music I wanted to hear I set off for my long day of providing for my family.

Thirteen hours and twenty-five minutes later the house was a wreck as if I didn't just clean up last night after working the same long hours. Jonelle was nowhere in sight. My feet were sore and my legs ached from all the walking at work, right now all I wanted to do was shower and get in bed.

Walking into the room I almost tripped over Jonelle's shoes that she had scattered all over the bedroom floor.

"Fuck!" I yelled out. She didn't pick up after herself at all.

Our four-year-old, Joy cleaned up and picked up more than she did. Looking at our king sized bed with the burgundy comforter set to match the curtains and décor of the room, there was no hope for me lying down in that bed unless I wanted to move all of her clothes off the bed. Stuff was everywhere and the pillows were on the floor. Both chairs had clothes in them so I couldn't even sit down. I looked around in disgust, this is not what I wanted to come home to every day after work.

The bayside window with the built-in seating and accent pillows where she loved to sit and read or look out the window daydreaming even had her dresses and shoes piled up in a heap. Walking to the closet I pushed the cracked door opened and I noticed that Jonelle's luggage was missing, as well as clothes pulled out and hung halfway. She didn't tell me she was going anywhere.

This was becoming a regular occurrence to come home to a dirty house or an empty one, usually, it was always both. To say I was pissed was an understatement. I didn't even bother to try to call Jonelle. I was tired.

I walked out of our bedroom closing the door behind me. Just as fast as I went into the bedroom I left out. There was no way in hell I was sleeping in that room tonight. I would sleep in the spare bedroom. Thankfully the room was clean.

As soon as my head hit the pillow I was out. Thankful that tomorrow was Saturday I could get some rest on my off day.

I woke up about ten to the doorbell ringing. Jonelle's mother Cherry was at the door with my baby Joy.

I was tired as hell from working overtime all week but I was always glad to see my sunshine.

"Come in Ms. Cherry."

I ushered her and my baby girl in. Joy ran to hug me; she was tall for her age. She looked like me and her mother.

"Hey, daddy." Joy hugged me then ran into her room and Cherry sat on the sofa.

I looked at my soon to be mother-in-law. Jonelle got her looks from her mother. She was the fifty-year-old who looked half her age. But one thing I will say she wasn't running around here wilding and acting like she was twenty-five. She didn't approve of the way her daughter carried on. We had many conversations about this, she wanted Jonelle to spend more time with me and her daughter.

"Hey, Zayvion. I would have kept Joy a little longer but I already made plans and I have to finish cooking for the church banquet tomorrow."

"It's okay. I thank you for watching her the way you do. I've been working all this overtime so I can have the money for the down payment on our house. I want it to be ready by our wedding date." I scratched my head. My barber had got me right the day before yesterday. My close cut was on point and to perfection.

Cherry smiled. "Jonelle has it made. You spoil her and Joy so much. I'm glad she has someone like you who loves her so much," she looked around the room. "Where is Jonelle anyway?"

"I don't know she wasn't here when I got here last night."

There was no point in lying.

Cherry's smile turned into a frown as she grabbed her purse and stood to leave.

"That girl is going to keep on messing up. Let me tell you Zayvion, I know you love my daughter but don't be a damned fool. You have a daughter that you need to think about as well."

Joy had returned to the living room, she had on the tv watching cartoons. Her long hair was braided in a Mohawk. She looked so cute sitting there. Cherry walked over to her and gave her a hug and a kiss. "Bye, grandma. Love you."

"Bye baby. Grandma loves you too." Cherry pointed her red

oval nails at me, with a serious expression on her face and said, "When she gets home please tell her to call me please Zayvion."

Joy stood up and walked with us to her grandmother's car. We stood on the sidewalk as she backed her SUV out and pulled out of the complex.

"Daddy, what we going do today? Where is mommy?"

I bent down to my daughter and gently pinched her chubby cheeks. I loved my baby girl so much. "Mommy will be home soon. If you be a good girl I'll take you to Sweet Frog later."

"You're the best daddy in the whole wide world. I will be good."

As we were going the short distance up the sidewalk I noticed Amika walking out of her apartment to her car. Following behind her was that buster ass fat clown boyfriend of hers, Jelly, a small time dope dealer. Rumor had it that he had two kids on her, I don't know how he even caught the attention of a girl like her. But for some reason, he was madly in love with him. She waved at us and he mean mugged from a distance. I was not wild and in the streets but I didn't take any shit from anybody so he had better fall back.

I spoke to her ignoring her clown ass boyfriend. Amika was a pretty redbone with freckles on her nose and cheeks. She was short and thick in all the right places. She also went to school with me and Jonelle. She was always the quiet shy type, yet she always would speak and make small talk. I don't think Jonelle cared too much for her but hey that was her problem. I didn't see any reason whatsoever to be rude. My only concern, for now, was to have a good day and have fun with my daughter.

CHAPTER 2 JONELLE

That's right baby. Eat that shit up. Suck my pussy like it's yours. I love it when Monster aka Zaddy ravished my kitty. I held my hand to the back of his head and grinded my hips feeding him this juicy twat until I became weak. I never ever should have asked this man "What that mouth do?"

Baby when I tell you he showed and proved. We had been together for a year and this was the best year of my life. I was down to ride for his fine ass all the way around. Right now I was speechless as he drained me from all that bomb mouth service he just provided. I arched my back and rode the wave hard as I came. His long tongue swirled in me. Zaddy had a tornado tongue.

Yes, I called him zaddy. He had swag and sex appeal.

Serving up good dick I had no choice but to call him daddy because he took care of this pussy, well zaddy because he left me speechless.

"Oh shit! Oh shit! Aghhhhh" I was cooing and gurgling. Almost chanting because he made me feel so good.

"Yes, baby!!!!!"

"That's right bust you another one baby. Cum for me."

I didn't give a shit who heard me get this good shit off as I concentrated on the sensations I was receiving as he strong-armed the pussy. With my ass against the sink, one leg on the floor and the other on the toilet holding on for the ride in the small bathroom while Monster was between my legs sucking and licking me into a frenzy. Did the room just change colors? Someone was twisting on the door trying to come in. Monster just kept on going. His long thick finger dipped in and out of me as his tongue swirled in and out slurping. I scooted away and tried to cover myself as if that would really cover me if someone came busting in. Fuck it let them catch us. This felt too good to stop.

I loved a thrill. That's why I fucked with him.

Not wanting to get caught but not giving a damn, the whole idea of being here turned me on.

After releasing myself for about the third time I had to push him off me to slide my panties back up. Anyone could walk in on us. Lucky for us the door was still locked.

My name is Jonelle Lynn Todd and I'm engaged.

By the end of the year, I'll be Mrs. Zayvion Black. Until then I'm just doing me and riding the wave of Monster. Catching my breath, I finally get it together. Monster stands back and just looks at me. He doesn't give a shit about anything. Zero fucks are given. All he wants is to eat it up and beat it up.

The knocking continues on the other side of the door. We are both unbothered. After tiring of hearing the banging, I yell out "Wait a fucking minute damn!"

This was not the only bathroom so I don't know what the fuck the problem was anyway. Somebody just wanted to be worrisome or see something.

"Next time I want that pussy don't make me wait." Rubbing his hands like he's Birdman he licks his big lips that were just drenched in my sweet juices.

Shit is happening too fast. This was never supposed to happen.

Monster is my best friend Neenah's brother. He knew I was damn near married with a kid.

So did I.

It was something about the nigga that made me want to get with him in the worse way.

Really light skin with a bald head and beard I had to have him. His bad boy tats were a turn on as well. Every time I saw him he looked like he just came out the mall. Only home for a year, all the bitches wanted him. I quickly locked him down, though. He only messed with bad bitches and he chose me. It was because of him that I stayed in some online beef. Lucky for me nobody ever brought this to my man, Zayvion's attention.

Washing his face and brushing his teeth Monster walked over to me and kissed me and slapped me on my ass.

Whoever it was on the other side of the door would just have to wait.

I was falling in love for this nigga. He had me ready to leave the one I was with and start a relationship with him. I wanted to be with him so bad I would have left Zay and Joy so quick. I don't know if it would work but I damn sure would be willing to try my hand. I washed off at the sink and fixed my clothes up. All I wanted to do now was go to sleep after the session we just had.

As soon as this kickback was over I was carrying my ass to bed. Ain't no going home tonight. Zayvion good and Joy is with my mom.

The first person I see when I leave out the bathroom is Moni. A bitch who makes my ass hurt. She's smiling showing those dingy ass golds. I hated her conniving thottin' ass. This bitch had me beat she wanted to be me so damn bad.

Grabbing my bag, I switched past her. Moni didn't have shit on me so she had better recognize.

Following closely Monster was on ass. Slapping me on the behind he couldn't keep his hands off me. The look on her face was priceless. She never expected to see the both of us walk out together.

Back in the living room, the party was live. The room was smoky from everyone smoking and there was plenty of alcohol. There was an assortment of drugs and I was ready to get it in. Neenah's house was the party spot. She would have these little get togethers on the regular.

Walking into the kitchen I was ready to make me a plate.

"Hold up, wait a minute bitch where you just coming from with that stupid ass smile on your face? Monster?"

Neenah put her drink down and jumped up from the card table playing spades with a cigarette in hand she grabbed her red cup filled with liquor.

"Sam play my hand!" She damn near threw her cards in his lap.

He was one of her cousins, Monster's younger brother, who always tried to holler at me but he always gets shut down, not that he was ugly but his money was not long enough to see me. I wasn't fucking with his ass. He looked at me in disgust. Fuck him.

Monster walked behind me. "Fix me a plate Jonelle."

Twisting her neck with her hands on her hips she stood in front of Monster.

"What the fuck is this shit? Yall niggas fucking around and

shit? Is she making plates? Um, what did I miss?"

He smiled showing a mouth full of gold teeth. Damn, he was sexy. "Neenah why you all in my damn business. Yeah, that's my boo."

I smiled and made his plate. That's all I needed to hear.

Sam slammed the cards on the table after winning the hands he was dealt. Personally, I think he was a little salty about me and Monster. Across the room, another hater looked on at me in envy.

CHAPTER 3 AMIKA

I can't believe that Jelly is so petty. Looking at my phone reading the text message in disbelief I get so sick of the fat bastard son of a bitch. Here I was waiting outside at work for him to pick me up and he was being trifling. Lucky for me it was not hot nor cold outside since he had me out here just waiting like a dumb ass.

Bzzzz. Bzzzzz. Bzzzzzzz.

My phone vibrated louder and louder. Upset I read the message that scrolled across the screen.

You should know how your man likes to be blessed. Next time do what I ask you!!!

He really had the nerve and audacity to say this to me. He was really asking me for some unrealistic mess and expecting me to say yes. On top of the fact that he was not here with my car to pick me up on time.

Jelly picking me up late was getting to be a regular occurrence. Looking at my watch here it was almost 7:30 pm and my shift at the daycare ended at 6! Today was going to be the day that I went off on him.

Tired of patiently waiting, I couldn't wait any longer, I was ready to get home. All my co-workers had already left. Like a fool, I turned down rides from the few people that would have dropped me off, confident and assured that he would be here to pick me up soon. As if things couldn't get any worse, Lauryn walked out with Sanya and Melissa on her tail. Headed towards her vehicle with her nose in the air and her eyes to the side looking at me, Lauryn was my boss and they were her followers. Kissing ass may have gotten them a bigger paycheck but I could care less at her or them. Those wishy washy chicks would be nice to me when she wasn't around but the moment she came around they seemed to forget they had a damn brain. Because of simple minded females like them, I chose to stick to myself. I hated drama and conflict.

Right now I wished I were invisible or could be standing anywhere but here. The same outfit that I thought I was killing it in when I got dressed this morning, now suddenly didn't feel so cute as I looked at Lauryn's slim thick body dressed a little too sexy to be working in a preschool/daycare setting. She knew she had it going on so she tried to make others feel like shit.

Lauryn clearly didn't care that I heard her when she let out the remark, "I would never let a man drive my damn car to work. Some bitches are dumb as hell."

Her two followers laughed. I wanted to check all three of them but I know I needed my job so I pretended not to hear them, listening to music with my headphones in my ears to drown out their ugly laughter as they got in their cars pulling away for the day.

Ugh, I wanted to say something so bad. I was not a confrontational chick so I put it to the back of my mind and checked again to see where my ride was.

Looking at my watch time was steady passing. I needed to be getting home. I was tired as hell. Jelly's phone now went

35

straight to voicemail. I could not believe his ass. Looks like I would be catching a cab home again today. I had just got one two days ago.

Feeling inside my purse I didn't feel my wallet. Just great. I forgot and left it at home when he was rushing me out the front door this morning.

He had some balls.

His ass didn't have a job because he could not seem to keep one for the life of him. I guess he was allergic to making money. I say that to say even though he didn't have a job he didn't have a hustle or any other means of getting money.

My name is Amika Cherie Carter. I'm so in love with Jelly. His real name is James Reid. He got the nickname Jelly because when he was a kid his greedy ass used to crush some jelly sandwiches so the name stuck. He was my baby and I was so gone over his love but sadly his love for me does not run deep for me the way my love does for him. At one point when I was really digging him, I had him saved in my phone as "My Oxygen" because loving him gave me life. It's funny how things change, though.

Sometimes I wonder if he even loves me at all. I've been riding for my man since day one but it seems like maybe he parked the car and said fuck it. There's nothing I won't do for Jelly and he knows this. I accept all his flaws because that's what a good woman does. I'd like to say I believe in real love. I just wanted this to be the real deal love I always dreamed about.

I got up this morning in a good mood, ready to have a good day. I jumped out the shower smelling fresh like sweet strawberries and champagne like my favorite body wash. It would have been nice had Jelly came ate me up like a strawberry but that wasn't happening. I'll tell you all about that in a minute, though.

He laid his husky, chunky ass in bed snoring all loudly, damn near ready to wake the apartment complex as I slid my neatly pressed, khaki pants on with the matching red polo shirt. I worked as a teacher a daycare. I loved my job, that was one reason I got up each day with a smile on my face and ready to conquer the day. For the last, for years I had been teaching the four and five-year-old class. I loved my kids and hoped to one day have children of my own. Me and Jelly had talked about that before but he wasn't ready for any kids with me yet.

After dressing I looked in the mirror so I could tame this mane. I didn't want to disturb Jelly but I had to find my hairspray so I could style my hair. I flicked on the light to grab what I needed to take with me to the bathroom.

"Turn the damn light off Amika!" He roared from under the cover. I seemed to be the only person he turned to a vicious lion with because he did not talk that big boy shit to anybody in the streets. I learned this nigga was a straight pussy and he only talked all this extra shit to me.

Yet I stayed with him. I was hoping that he would one day boss up. Maybe it was nothing but some hope. I didn't want to be seen as one of those females that didn't stick by her man I wanted us to build and work things out. Three years in and I think we were on the right path.

"Ok babe. Love you, Jelly."

I constantly reassured him that I loved him.

With his head still under the cover, breathy he said, "You too."

His fat ass talked like he was always at a loss of breath, breathing all shallow like any moment he was going to lose all his oxygen. I was used to it by now. He may have had the Rick Ross look but he sure didn't have that sound. Looks really could be deceiving. The nerve of him to roll back under the damn blanket like it wasn't time for him to get up.

Smiling I grabbed my spray and went into the bathroom to style my hair. I wore my natural hair in a big red curly afro. Every now and then I would wear blowouts but I loved my curls. It was very becoming plus the red highlighted my skin. Satisfied with my look I hurried so I could make breakfast. Jelly loved for me to cook him breakfast each morning. Let's just keep it real he loved any meal I cooked whether it be breakfast, lunch or dinner. Hopefully, he would have his shit together by the time I got finished.

"What the hell!" I yelled out loud as if someone was in the room with me. Un-freaking-believable. I stopped singing my favorite song by Beyoncé, I was almost ready to put in some early morning work in the kitchen when I opened the freezer to pull out some meat when I noticed that the freezer was empty.

My mouth dropped.

Slamming the door shut I stood with my back against the freezer in pure disbelief. I needed a minute or two. Slapping the pack of bacon on the cold amber colored granite counter I no longer had a desire to cook anything. I just made groceries last week when I got paid. This shit was getting very old.

The only thing in the damned freezer was a half-filled ice tray of stale ice, some diet popsicles and some beef liver, and this package of turkey bacon. All that food that I got last week was gone. My eyes had to be deceiving me.

Jelly was not going to get away with this shit today.

"Jelly!" I yelled loud enough to wake the neighbors.

Right now I didn't give a rat's ass if I woke the whole damn city. This fool had some explaining to do. When I buy food I buy it for the entire month so that I don't have to do so again. All my money was accounted for since he never had any money to contribute to shit around here. I couponed and I budgeted my funds because I was saving my money up. He was in the damn way.

Huffing and puffing like the big bad wolf Jelly waddled his big ass in the kitchen with nothing on but boxers. He used to be a sexy big guy now his ass was just a big guy. He could have put them damn moobs or mitties under a shirt. That what I called his man boobs or man titties. I told you he was letting this Rick Ross image go to his damn head. Men were quick to talk about how women would let themselves go but he was damn sure proof that some men didn't give a flying fuck once they had you in a relationship.

"The fuck you doing all that yelling for! It's too early for you to be acting all stupid and shit. This why I hate being at home now."

Stepping back, I put my hands on my hips. Here he was with crust in his eyes talking junk. Wash your damn face and brush your teeth before raising your voice to me. I hated him being at home too. He was always being a jerk. I could live without it. Trying not to go completely to the left I took a deep breath.

"Whatever... Where is all our food at? Did the food disappear? I mean please, explain to me."

"Don't question me in my house."

We stood eye to eye. Jelly was not ugly his ways were. Initially, I loved the fact that he was my big cuddly teddy bear now that fool was nothing but a damn grizzly bear in my eyes. Sucking my teeth and growing more frustrated by the second I said, "I just want to know why it's not a damn thing in the freezer. I spent all that money and its nothing but a funky ass pack of liver in here."

I snatched the door open so he could see it with his own two eyes. Maybe the food would reappear.

"Oh yeah. I meant to tell you baby mama ain't have no food for Niya and Rell."

While I was standing there clearly pissed off, Jelly pulled out a big mixing bowl and dumped it full of my cereal, ignoring me. I always ate frosted flakes and a banana. He didn't eat cereal because I always made him breakfast. He gave away all the meat. He didn't deserve to eat anything in this bitch.

"Ok, that does not explain why we don't have any food in here."

It pisses me off to watch him pour my ice cold almond milk into the bowl, lactose intolerant, that's the type of milk I prefer.

Taking the first big bite he looks up at me before walking to the counter. I just watch him. I'm not cooking jack and I'm not buying anything else in this bitch.

Scarfing the cereal down, he's chewing and smacking loudly before he can speak.

"Amika... boo. I know you not mad. You not going see my lil man and my princess hungry are you?"

He loves to bring up the kids because he knows that I have a soft spot for them. I want my own children in the worse way but until we have a baby then I will settle for loving on his four and five-year-old son and daughter.

"Naw but I made sure to pay your child support. What is Jacquee doing with her food stamps or child support for that matter?"

Every month I would pay his child support. I would split the payments up when I got paid and drop them off at DCSE so his ass wouldn't get locked up. I didn't want to see my man in jail.

Almost done with his food Jelly is still smacking on the cereal as he looks over at me.

"Don't question me about Jacquee. She a grown ass woman. You don't like her. You've made that clear time and time again. All you need to know is that my seeds were hungry. You need to get on board with the program or get left behind."

"You get on my nerves. I'm not going to argue with you. I'm going have a good day at work and I'm coming home to chill. Simple as that."

"That's my girl."

There was no point in me going back and forth with him about the situation. I didn't have time to go through this with Jelly and be late for work this morning. He went into the bathroom and took care of his hygiene so we could leave. I had been on time for the last month or so since Lauryn, who could be a bitch sometimes wrote me up. As much as I loved my job I could not stand her so I didn't want to get on her bad side. She had been nothing but annoying since she got the job, regardless of what I did lately she always had a slick comment or remark to make. To make a long story short about my boss, her father was the owner of the daycare. When she moved from Maryland, he gave her the position. I should have gone to me. She knew that as well so she reminded me every chance that she got that she was my boss. Me being the woman I am, I kept a positive attitude and ignored her for the most part.

***

Tidying up the living room a bit, I had a moment to think. I couldn't stand his whoring baby mama Jacquee. This tired broad was almost forty if not already forty with six kids and five baby daddies. My dumb ass man just happened to be the father of her last two. I had no respect for her because she spread her legs and got not one but two babies by my man.

She was a stone cold freak. All she wanted to do was party and show off. Jacquee was the type of female that had kids but expected the fathers to provide everything for them. Any and everything those kids had me and Jelly paid for, and then she would be quick to get on FB or Snapchat talking about the shit like she broke some bread. I paid his child support because she threatened to have his ass put in jail the moment those checks didn't come through. This lady was a piece of work. I swear I couldn't stand her. She was too old for her shit.

Speaking of old her name wasn't even Jacquee, pronounced Jock-Qwee, it was Jackie but she thought that made her sound old being called Jackie. I couldn't deal! I always thought you called a spade a spade and a thot at thot. I guess not dealing with her.

And on that note here she was with a twenty-seven-year-old baby daddy and she was forty or older.

In the living room, I was clipping coupons the night before so and I had my wallet at my desk when I was paying a few bills. Hell, I was the only one that ever did that around here. I hoped this day went by quickly. I could see now things were getting off to a bad start.

"Come on Amika damn. I don't have all morning to mess around with you. And stop acting childish about the food. I'll put it back. I got us."

I walked through the house one more time to make sure I did everything I needed to do before leaving out, grabbing my purse, I was ready to get to work. Fuck Jelly and his stupid baby mama. They would not consume my thoughts. I knew this mess that me and him had going on could not be love. There had to be more for me in the love department than this.

Sinking into the passenger seat I fastened my seatbelt and thought about what love should be. I swear it felt like me and this nigga was going through the motions. Looking at him bopping to the music he really seemed unbothered while my ass was unhappy. He either didn't notice or didn't care.

The ride to work didn't take long. Jelly drove my late model Acura, pushing it through the city like it was his was the seat laid back. I had a lot to think about. Nevertheless, I would never take my problems to work. He pulled me up to the front door and I leaned over towards him for a kiss on the lips and he gave me the lamest kiss. I was not going to dwell on that either. It hurt a little because of course, my nosey ass coworkers were going in, around the same time. I put a smile on my face and went to make my day.

***

Jelly had been asking me to have a threesome with him and Jacquee. I don't think he understood that no meant no. He honestly never should have fixed his face to ask me some shit

47

like that in the first place but since he did I made sure to cuss his ass out   He texted me while I was at work and of course I told him to kiss my ass, just like that. I was not into women and even if I ever was the slight bit curious Jacquee couldn't touch me ever in life. Her kitty cat did not have any restrictions; she gave it away freely.

I was getting a headache thinking about this stupid ass shit. If he thought, I told him off in those text message he was really in for it when I got home. I was going to curse Jelly out so good face to face.

I planned to have a good distraction free day. Sorry for me, it didn't work out that way. Between him texting me all day trying to set up a ménage with his baby mama and Lauryn coming at me with extra tasks, and things that I swear were not in my job description, I was ready to go home and soak in the tub and just relax with a drink. I didn't even drink!

A getaway from work and him would have done me just fine. I couldn't afford to go anywhere right now though because school had just started so a nice bath and wine would have to do. Because I didn't want to act out his nasty, trifling fantasy he chose not to pick me up on time. He was ready to see a whole new side of me.

***

When the cab pulled up to my building the first car I see in the parking lot was mine. I was going to hurt Jelly when I got in the house. He could have picked me up. I paid the driver and got out. I was seeing red as I walked up to the door.

I rehearsed my cuss out in my head for what I was going to say to him. I wanted him to know that I was not playing with him.

I could hear the television turned up full blast with Madden 2017, sounding like a real football game was taking place.

Sitting on the edge of the chair with the phone to his ear and the PS4 controller in hand Jelly was playing the game. He looked mighty comfortable. It was evident that he had no intentions of picking me up.

I walked directly in front of him and cut the tv off right in the middle of the game.

"So you couldn't come get me because you in here playing the damn game!"

I did not care if I messed his game system up as I went further and unplugged the power cord.

"Let me call you back my nigga. Amika just came in here wit' the shits."

He laughed into the phone to whoever he was talking to. I'm sure it was one of his equally broke ass homeboys.

"Yeah get off the phone and talk to me dammit!"

"Amika take your ass on somewhere and stop playing wit' me shit. You doing too much."

With my hands on my hips, I stood my ground.

"Jelly you're not doing enough! You won't keep a job. You suck at your piss poor attempt at selling drugs. I could keep going with this!"

"Oh, that's how you feel. See if you feel like I do enough when I leave your ass in here by yourself. Your weak ass can't make it without me. You need me."

I didn't really expect him to leave until I saw him go in the room and get his shoes. He showed my ass. He picked up my car keys and headed for the door.

"Where are you going Jelly?"

He kept on walking.

I wanted to run behind him and fight and some more foolishness but I didn't want to go outside showing my ass in front of my neighbors. I was not that type of female. I had appearances to make.

I wanted the world to believe that I had all my stuff together. I had a good job and a good man. Well, I had a man. He was not that good to me but that was not anything that everyone needed to know.

Who was I fooling, everyone knew that Jelly was trifling as hell. I stayed with him because I didn't want to be alone. He was what I was used to. When we got together he was sweet and attentive and loving. He was everything that I wanted in a man. Well, come to think of it, he wasn't.

He used to buy me nice gifts and take me out and we would have fun. Jelly had hopes and dreams and I loved that about him. I found out over the years that he was all talk and no action.

He used to say he wanted to start his own business and he

wanted to go back to school. He didn't want to do but the bare minimum that he was doing. I knew that he was capable of doing so much more and that's why I stayed with him.

It was Friday night and I was cooped up in the house alone while Jelly was out god knows where doing god knows what. I would have called up a friend but I didn't have any after investing so much time into my relationship. I really didn't have anyone to talk to. The one friend I did have, Monica, Jelly made sure to cause problems with us. After waiting up Jelly he never came back home.

Spent from waiting on Jelly to return home I crawled into bed alone. It was nothing new to me. When he was out creating his kids I spent many nights in bed alone crying my eyes out. I'm confident he was back up to his old tricks. It was hard trying to sleep with a broken heart. After tossing and turning most of the night sleep finally found me.

Just as soon as I found a comfortable place in bed I felt the sun beaming through the tall windows, shining down on me. The smell of bacon and freshly brewed coffee filled my nostrils, making my mouth water. Immediately I got up.

Rushing into the bathroom I took care of my hygiene.

I could not believe the sight before my eyes. Jelly had breakfast laid out for me. He picked up breakfast from a diner on his way home and he whipped out my K-cups and used my Keurig to make my coffee.

"Good morning sleepy head. You were knocked out when I got back so I went back out and got you something to eat."

I grabbed my container of food and went into the living room area to watch tv. I took a seat on the sofa, pulling the cocktail table closer to eat. Jelly plopped down on the chair next to me.

"Look I'm sorry for trippin' on you earlier. I mean it from the bottom of my heart Amika. I didn't mean to upset you earlier."

I piled two strips of turkey bacon into my mouth. It was really thick and crispy. I smacked when I ate. Jelly looked at me. I guess I was taking away from his apology.

"Ok."

I opened my grits and added sugar, salt, and pepper. Stirring them, they were just right now.

"Amika are you paying me any attention?"

Jelly still wore the same clothes that he had on when he left. I wondered where he went when he left out of here.

"Yes. I'm listening. I shouldn't listen. How many times are we going to keep doing shit and apologizing? The words mean absolutely nothing if we not going act on it! How many times have you told me you were sorry or that you loved me but you turn around and go back to the same shit?"

"Listen to me. That was in the past. I don't want to keep going back and forth with you baby. Before you say anything else, I put all the food back that you were bitching about."

Sipping my black coffee, I almost spilled it. I loved my coffee like my men dark. I didn't want to waste a drop of it. I had already wasted my time, damn if I needed to waste this cup of joe.

"I know damn well you didn't go get the food out of Jacquee's freezer? I don't want shit from her. Oh, my god, you took food from the kids?"

He pursed his lips. "Calm down. I just came up on some stuff, so I was able to go buy more food. I told you I was going to take care of business, didn't I?"

It was hard to believe but he did say that. I don't know where he got money from or what he had going on so I was going to leave that alone. Whatever he did I did not want it coming back to kick me in my ass later. Before he thought he was off the hook I set him straight. I had been holding this in since he left. Now it was time to get it off my chest.

"Well now that that issue is resolved let's talk about this other thing."

He already knew what I was talking about.

"Oh lord. Why you gotta keep bringing old shit up. You will not let shit die, will you? What do I have to do for you to stop riding me so much?"

I looked at him like he was crazy.

"Riding you? Bringing up old shit? You got some nerve. You have continued to ask me to fuck your baby mama with you. I mean where the fuck do they do that at Jelly?"

"And I said never mind."

"You damn right you said never mind. I'm not gay and that shit will never happen. So get it out of your head. You lucky I didn't cut you off for asking me something like that."

"Just forget I ever asked you. It was just a thought. I just wanted to spice up our sex life."

The only thing that could spice up our sex life is if Jelly removed himself from it. He was not doing anything for me in the bedroom. He wasn't bossing up in the sex game and here he wanted to recruit a third party. He should have been ashamed but he wasn't.

"Let's just be clear Jelly. I can forgive you but I will not forget. We have history and I want us to work. You are not in the clear but I'm willing to work on us."

"Things going get better around here real soon. You will see. Why don't you get dressed so we can go out for a little while?"

I don't know when the last time we went somewhere as a couple so I got my shit together, quick, fast and in a hurry before he changed his mind. I threw on some jeans and a cute top.

When we got outside I spied my fine neighbor, Zayvion and his daughter Joy, in the parking lot. He would always speak but his mean girlfriend's hood, bougie self never spoke. I didn't want her man. I had my own. She would grab him all close and shit when she would see me. I noticed Jelly didn't say too much to Zayvion or how he'd never speak. He was just as foolish as Jonelle. I guess she felt slim thick could take her man, with her bony ass. I didn't need nor do drama. Jelly got in driver's side and we were on our way.

CHAPTER 4 ZAYVION

Anything my baby girl wants my baby girl gets. I let Joy play herself out when we went to the park. After running around and playing on the swings she tired herself out. After going to the park I took her favorite place, Sweet Frog, to get frozen yogurt as promised for being a good girl. I cherished these moments that I spent with my daughter. Too bad her own mother didn't. Jonelle would rather hang out and be seen than be a mother to the beautiful princess we created. After having a fun filled day with my daughter it was now evening. All we did was go to the mall and to the park and the day was almost over. My baby was asleep in the car before we even made it home. I was glad she was out; I could finally try to catch up on my rest.

Looking at Joy sleep in her room, she was my life. She would never know anything about the half ass mothering that Jonelle put down.

Speaking of her, she texted me once last night.

Bae, I'm out with Neenah. Be home soon 💋♥️☐

That explained a whole lot. I hated when she hung out with Neenah's bad news ass. She meant no good. Jonelle could not see that her single friend wanted her to be single just as bad as she was. Neenah had tried to make a pass at me before but just as fast as she tried it I dismissed her. I was not a grimy dude and there was nothing about her worth risking my woman or family for. If Jonelle knew how messy and envious her girl was she would not stick so close to her. Her ass would learn one day.

While baby girl slept I decided to watch a little tv. I may even take a nap as well since I had worked long hours all week. It was still early so I would get up later after catching a nap. ESPN was watching me before I knew it.

I was slumped over on the sofa, getting that good rest, the

kind where you are snoring extra loud and drool forms in the corner of your mouth. I was dog tired.

My hard work was going to pay off. I was busting my ass to pay this house that Jonelle wanted. A brother was so tired that I dreamed about work. In my dream, I was monitoring the employees and doing evaluations at the mega store distribution center where I worked. I was just about to check to see did the people make production when I was interrupted by the break bell, which rang out loud like the bells that we used to have in school that signaled when it was time to switch classes.

With creases in my face from the throw pillow on the chair, I sat up. I was not at work. I was at home on the sofa and it was just my phone going off, vibrating next to the pillow. Without checking to see who was on the other line I answered.

"You have a collect call from an inmate at Riverside Regional Jail."

Who the hell was in jail? I could hear a whole lot of commotion in the background and an echo like the person was in a large room. My first thought was to hang up until I heard her deep voice say, "Jonelle".

Immediately I jumped up no longer fatigued. I was amped all the way up. I pressed five to accept so fast I had to make sure that I didn't disconnect the call. She had a cussing out coming her way. Why the hell was my soon to be wife and baby mother in jail?

"Hello…. Zay. Say something!"

I didn't know what to say. The last thing I heard from her was that she was with Neenah. How did she go from that to jail? Before I could say anything else she was telling me what I needed to do to get her out and to hurry.

"Can you please come and get me? I'll explain everything when you pick me up."

I really wanted to be mad at Jonelle but I couldn't be. She had never been to jail before so she was probably scared.

"I'm on my way to get you right now."

With a sigh of relief, she said, "Thanks, Zay. You are a life saver. Please don't tell mama that I'm here."

"Why not?"

"Look, baby, just please come and get me. We will talk when

you get me. My mom would trip if she knew I was here so she does not need to know."

I was not about to go back and forth with her so I did what she asked and got ready to come get her. I looked at my sleeping princess. I didn't want to wake Joy. She didn't need to go down to the jail with me and her grandmother was doing her dinner sales today so it was out of the question to take her to Cherry anyway. I got an idea.

I changed my clothes out of the sweats that I had on because Jonelle hated when I wore those out. She said that she didn't want other chicks looking at her eggplant as she loved to say. That girl was crazy as fuck. After washing my face and brushing my teeth, I put on some jeans woke Joy up.

Grabbing up her backpack and a few snacks and a few of her toys, with her still sleep in my arms I took her across the parking lot to Amika. Well simply because Joy loved Amika. She was her teacher when she was in the three-year-old class and she always said if I needed her to watch my baby she would. Today was that day I was calling in on that favor. Knocking on the door I hoped that she was home. I only needed her to watch her for about an hour or two at the most.

I didn't mean to bang on her door but I guess I knocked a little too loud or too hard. Amika snatched the door open with an attitude. Her hair was in a big red puff ball and she had earphones in her ears with a long paintbrush in hand.

Even with a scowl on her face, she was fine as hell.

"Jelly why the hell you didn't use your damn house key…."

She was ready to give that nigga a verbal lashing. I smiled at her.

"Hey, Amika."

My eyes roamed over all that thickness. I don't know if she knows it but she was beautiful melanin goddess. She wore an oversized shirt with some tiny shorts that showed off her thick thighs. She had paint on her shirt and hands. I guess she could feel me looking at her because she that anger and fire that she snatched the door open with subsided. I don't know what the hell her man was doing to fuck up but with a woman like her a man needed to be on their shit at all times. A woman like her was the kind of woman that a brother wanted to give her all to. Here I was lusting over her with my child in my arms, on my way to pick Jonelle up from jail.

What kind of mess was this?

"I thought for a minute you were Jelly. But then again, I should have known that he would not be back home anytime soon. Come on in."

She led the way to her living room and continued talking, "What's up Zayvion? You were ready to beat my door down and you got lil' mama in your arms?" Since she was leading the way my eyes followed her ass as she walked in front of me, you would have to be a blind man not to notice her body. It was something about the way she carried herself.

Without even asking I laid Joy on her sofa and put her bag down.

"I need you to do me a favor. Can you please watch her for me?" I looked up at her.

Amika washed her hands. She spoke over the water running.

"Yeah sure no problem. You know I've been telling you to bring her by here for the longest. I was just in here painting. As you can see. I'll watch her for you.

The red, and orange paints looked good against her skin. I

wish I could be that paint that close to her. I would love to stroke her the way she had stroked her paintbrushes skillfully against the canvas. We could create beautiful art. A masterpiece.

Looking at the piece she was working on I was highly impressed. I never knew that she was so talented. The easel with her work held an autumn amazement. She had captured the beauty of the season with paint. One felt like they were right there on a fall day. She had skills.

"Thanks so much you are a lifesaver girl. I could hug you and kiss you but you got paint all over yourself. Amika you have skills."

"Stop it," she laughed.

She just doesn't know I could have wrapped my arms around her and picked her up. Looking at those thick meaty thighs I wanted nothing more than to scoop her up and grab her soft booty. I had to hurry up and get out of here. I knew Jonelle was a bad chick but today seeing her in her element just being herself that made me want to know more about her and really got my attention.

She walked me to the door. I really wanted to hug her for agreeing to watch Joy at the last minute.

"Thanks, Amika. I'll be back soon."

***

Riverside Regional Jail was not where I wanted to be on my off day. I stood looking at the place that held my fiancé captive for a little while. I wondered what the hell could she have done to landed herself here. I couldn't believe this girl. She had better have a damn good reason why her ass got arrested. While playing with my phone the bails bondsmen who I spoke with on the phone pulled up beside me. After quick introductions, we both went inside.

I had to sign all kinds of papers making myself responsible for Jonelle. She had to show up to court and shit like that. I was just ready for her to show up now.

The entire process of getting her out took about two hours itself. As patient as I am, I can't stand a negative Nancy or an impatient motherfucker. The moment I signed the papers and Jonelle got into the car she was off the chain.

First of all, I waited all night for her to show up at home. Now she was in a hurry to get home.

I put on my seat belt and started the engine. Before I could pull out the parking lot Jonelle wanted to show her monkey ass. "It's about time! What took you so long Zayvion damn? I need to go over Neenah's house to get my stuff."

She reclined her seat and placed her big movie star dramatic shades over her eyes. The huge glasses hid dark circles from an obvious night of partying. I barely recognized her without makeup caked and slathered on her thin face.

She wore tight jeans that made her almost non-existent booty appear to be bigger with red high heels that any working woman would not have time to worn. I'm sure those shoes probably added up to twice our monthly living expenses times two. She was dressed like she was ready to rip some kind of hip hop runway or be one of those bougie girls in the video.

She had on a white camisole and her jewelry hung off her bony wrist and her chains fell right between her small chest.

I looked at her in disbelief. No thanks or anything. When she got in the car and didn't see her daughter she didn't even inquire about her so I brought Joy to her attention, reminding her that she was a mother.

Speaking slowly through clenched teeth I emphasized each word so she would understand me. "I got here as fast as I could. I didn't want to bring Joy with me to a jail.

You didn't even ask about your only child all you are worried about is some shit that you left at your girl house."

"Zay this is important. Trust me."

I hit the steering wheel with my fist. This got Jonelle's attention. For too long I had been quiet letting her have her say and her way.

"What could be more important than your daughter? Had you had your ass at home last night we wouldn't be sitting here right now. Any and everything else right now is irrelevant to me. We are going to pick up our daughter and we are going home as a family. You run the streets like you don't have shit at home."

She sat there with her mouth open. I had taken her by surprise which left her speechless. I didn't want to hear shit she had to say right now so her best bet was to lay back in the seat and ride, once we got home we would talk.

I arrived at my designated spot and parked the car.

"What time is mama bringing Joy home? I hope I have time to take a shower before she drops her off. I thought we were picking her up anyway?" She looked puzzled.

"She's not."

"Come again? Well, what time are we going to get her? I'm ready to wash my ass and relax!"

"I was in a rush to get you so I left her with Amika."

Jonelle leaned her neck so hard she almost bent it. "You left my baby where, Zayvion?"

"Amika, who lives across from us. Light skin with red hair, Amika, that we went to school with."

"Why the fuck you leave my daughter with that bitch? I can't believe this! You must be fucking her! I'm not stupid. The ho won't play mama to mine!"

Jonelle jumped out of the car slamming the door hard, with her shoes in her hands. She was headed for Amika's door. She wanted to be a billy bad ass I hoped she didn't go barking up the wrong tree and get her ass kicked.

"Jonelle!!! Come back here. I'll go get Joy. Wait up. I'm

69

coming."

I was right behind her. She reached the door yelling and screaming "Amika is a whore!!!!"

Did this fool think she was Karen, from Goodfellas? In any other circumstances, I would have laughed but it was not a laughing matter with her making a public scene. I tried to grab her to stop her from kicking the door. She kept on banging and screaming, "Amika open the fucking door. I see you looking homewrecker!"

Looking like a breath of fresh air Amika opened her door calmly.

"Jonelle I'm going to ask you nicely to get the fuck away from my door. Your child is in here sleeping for one thing. Here you are acting like ghetto trash. But that's typical thot behavior. That's your style. Leave now before I have your ass escorted away."

"You don't tell me what the hell to do! Just get my baby so she can go home. I'm going home to my man. My family. Get your own fucking man!"

Amika didn't seem to be scared or backing down from Jonelle.

"I'm not going to ask you again to leave. Get the fuck away from my door."

I stepped between the two.

"Jonelle please just go in the house. I will get Joy. Please."

That really set her off.

"Yeah, Zay you are fucking her! You going send me away for her. And why she watching our daughter?"

I had it up to the ceiling with Jonelle. "Just go the fuck home."

Now was Amika's turn to speak. "If you were taking care of this happy home and spending time with your daughter she wouldn't be over here with me? Why didn't you watch your own child? Unfit ass."

That put Jonelle in her place. She no longer had any fight in her. She walked away angry. She didn't have a comeback for that.

Now that Jonelle was gone my attention was on Amika. I smiled weakly at her. I feared that she would curse me out for bringing drama to her door.

"Don't look at me all stupid smiling and shit Zayvion. I do you a favor and this is the thanks I get. Let me get Joy. I don't have shit to say to you."

I tried to sneak a peek at her backside as went to get my princess. She was sexy as hell. I tried to look the other way and pretend not to be staring at her when she returned with Joy in her arms and her bag. I don't know what Amika was doing to me. I had a woman and she had a man.

CHAPTER 5 JONELLE

Throwing my favorite shoes across the room I was furious. I know for a fact that Zayvion is fucking Amika. He took her side over mine. He made me go home! I can't believe this fuckery. He acts like he is so in love with me yet he is out here focused on the next female instead of me. I tell you guys sure could pretend. Well, I was going to show him two can play that game.

Then the nerve of Amika trying to go hard like he was her man. She'd better worry about Jelly and how he has her looking like a whole fool out here in the streets.

Trust me she didn't want it with me. I would hurt her little feelings for real. She better go pay his child support or watch those little bastards that he made on her. She was no competition for me on my worse day.

Pacing back and forth across the floor I wondered what was taking him so long to get back over here?

 The thought crossed my mind to go back over there, run up in the house and beat her ass to a pulp and deal with Zay later but I didn't want to end up right back in jail. Amika ol' scary ass would have pressed charges so fast, so I decided against it. She probably thought she had the last laugh but she didn't. Looking out the window, not giving a damn if they saw me move the blinds, I wanted to see if Zay was on the way, he still wasn't. His tall ass was just standing at the door looking simple. Probably over there pleading and shit because I messed up his little friendship. To hell with them both!

I put my phone on the charger and decided to check my phone to check my missed calls and messages. Scrolling through my phone I see that Monster and Neenah had been blowing my line up. The notifications were coming through back to back. It was Monster's fault that I got locked up in the first damn place.

Laid back on the passenger side he was pushing my BMW around with the music loud, smoking loud and my hair blowing in the wind. I was feeling all carefree.

Looking at the fine boss beside me, he was a young fly nigga.
He excited me like no other. I felt like I was on top of the world.
He had only been home for about a year from doing a bid and
I just had to have him. He put it out there like he was about his
money so I definitely wanted a piece of him. I was bored with
the day to day average shit at home. We had been sneaking
around behind everyone's back even Neenah's. It felt good to
finally come out about what we had going on. Everyone knew
me as Zay's fiancé but I was quick to tell them that Monster
was just my brother. Bitches were too damn nosey.

I wanted to read my messages and check my voicemail but I
didn't want to risk getting caught by Zay because any moment
now he would be back. I slipped the phone in my pocket and
looked back out the window. Amika's sloppy ass was bringing
Joy to the door in her arms. She gently placed her in Zay's
arms. I don't know why they were holding her like she was a
baby. I didn't have time to be carrying a big ass four-year-old
around. She'd better walk.

I know after Zayvion put his beloved daughter to bed he was

going to be on my ass like white on rice so I made my way to the bathroom.

I needed a shower and time to get my lies straight after sitting in jail all day, the story went way further than Monster driving my car around. Even though I may have complained about Zay and this family shit, I was not ready to mess anything up yet. I guess you could say I wanted my cake and it too.

Once I got in the bathroom I locked the door. I needed my privacy. I didn't need his ass walking in on me. Zayvion was good for that shit coming in the bathroom with me. We had two full bathrooms yet he had to invade my space. I just wanted to wash my ass in peace and check out my phone.

Stripping out of my clothes I didn't wear any underwear. Monster had ripped them off me earlier that day. I ran my water with bath salts so I could soak my body. At first, I was going to take a shower but then I decided to hell with it, I was not in a rush to talk to Zayvion. He made me wait on him at the jail and I was going to make him wait right now. He could put Joy to be and do whatever he needed to do before I came out.

Knock. Knock. Knock.

His voice rumbled through the door. "Jonelle! How long are you going be in the bathroom? That was messed up how you carried on at Amika's house just now. We need to talk. I don't have all night to wait on you."

That was the point.

"I'll be out soon. We can talk then."

I'm glad I locked the door. I couldn't even get clean in peace around here. An hour and thirty minutes later I came out of the bathroom. Hopefully, Zayvion would be asleep. It was late and him and Joy had church in the morning. We used to go every Sunday as a family but I cut my visits to the Lord's house back. I went maybe once or twice a month. I was not going because I had plans to sleep in. Usually, when my family was at church I would be giving the praises and glory to my zaddy, Monster. Sounds fucked up but that was just the way it was. He gave me life. One of these days when I got the courage to leave I was going just say to hell with it all and go be with him. Gathering my robe close to me, I walked lightly into the room I was hoping that he would be knocked out. Well, the devil was a liar. To my surprise, his ass was sitting on the bed with nothing on but boxers with his back turned to me watching the news. The masculine, refreshing scent of his body wash invaded my nostrils.

He turned and looked at me.

I smiled weakly at my fiancé before putting my hair scarf on. We were definitely way into this thing called a relationship. I didn't care how he saw me. When we first got together I did not want him to see me in a bonnet or hair scarf. His vision of me was to always be of beauty. Now that I had boyfriend number two I really didn't give damn, well I did just a little. I didn't want to have this conversation about jail or Amika so I decided to put on my charm. I was going still going to blast his ass about Amika later maybe even tomorrow but I was not going to get into the fiasco of getting arrested. I knew how to pick and choose my battles. That was one I didn't want.

I sat on the bed beside Zay. I was not sure how the conversation was going to go but I was going to come out on top. I was not above lying or sexing him to keep him from learning the truth. So I took the sweet approach.

"I'm ready to lay down Jonelle. You took your time in the bathroom."

"Well let's lie down then babe."

Pulling the covers back we got in bed and I got close to him hugging him. He couldn't resist me. I had his heart and his mind that's why he proposed to me.

"I'm really sorry Zayvion. Thanks for coming to get me. And thanks for always loving me. Love you."

I laid my head on his chest which and listened to his heartbeat. I felt at ease this close to him, even if I was trying to run game on him. It seemed like I was always telling him that I loved him. I can't say that I showed him. It was only now that I saw another woman looking at what was mine that I wanted to get it right.

"I love you too."

"I didn't mean to get crazy wit' ol girl but you gotta understand she wants you, Zay. I can see the way she be looking at you."

He rubbed my back. It felt damned good. I was getting sleepy myself now. If he kept this up I was going to be comatose immediately.

"You don't have to worry about her. You are the only woman for me. There is a not a woman alive that can take your place."

"I sure hope so. You're the only man for me. I don't mind checking a chick about my man you know that right."

He laughed. "Girl go to sleep. We will talk in the morning."

"Good night sweet dreams."

I kissed Zay on the lips and he kissed me back. For now, I had avoided the conversation. With sleep taking over I was ready for my dreams because somehow I felt that things were about to become a nightmare for me.

6 CHAPTER AMIKA

Just when I think everything is all good the ugly reality usually kicks in. About three weeks had passed since I had the weekend from hell. The one which Jelly gave away the groceries, didn't pick me up from work, he didn't come home and I had the run in with that undercover ho Jonelle.

After I went off, Jelly managed to replace the food and he apologized. I guess he realized that if he didn't get right he was going to get left. He was doing his best to make things up to me. What shocked me was the day he came home with a badge and a start date. I had just come from the library, after and he was home already. That in itself was a shock. He was never home much especially before it got dark outside.

"Hey, baby." He smiled up at me, he was filling out some forms. Upon closer inspection, I realized Jelly was sitting at the table filling out his employment paperwork.

"Hey, boo." He could tell by the pleased look on my face that I was happy for him.

"I know you see it. Your man got a job. I told you I was going to get back on my shit."

I ran over and hugged him. He embraced me and it felt good.

"I'm so proud of you Jelly. We gotta go out and celebrate."

"We can do that. What do you want to do or where do you want to go?"

"I don't care let's just get out!

That was a start for us going out doing something. I was back to loving my Jelly.

Jelly was working for a temp agency and had been contributing to bills. But then again, I guess it was no big deal since I had paid his child support up for him. Most people would think I was a fool for doing it but I was doing it in the name of love and I was doing it for the kids. They couldn't help how they got here.

Speaking of how the kids got here when I went to the nail

salon who did I bump into other than Jacquee. It was payday week and I was out pampering myself then going to do a little retail therapy. She was in there with her loud friend Moni. Once I was finishing up my pedicure and on my way to the table to get my manicure they walked in. I was surprised she was acting civil and cordial, it was at one time that she used to pick and try to give me hell. I mean she was forty going on fifty so she should have always been the more mature older woman in the situation. That was clearly not the case with this old bird. I guess her old ass had turned over a new leaf.

Jacquee wore a long lace frontal wig and it was styled with the curls going to the side. She actually wore something that covered her body today. She had on all black crop top with her gut exposed. She could stand to do a few sit ups. Her matching joggers with Moschino wrote in pink all over spread across her wide backside. The designer outfit looked like a cheap knockoff set she had purchased from some at home boutique. I myself would rather have on something nice and inexpensive that I could afford instead of some flashy counterfeit designer clothes. She thought she was killing em' so I decided to let her live.

I spoke and kept it moving. I was not a drama filled female. I went to my nail tech Paris, who was an associate. I didn't use the word friend too loosely because females these days were so unpredictable. I had been coming to her since this location, Lovely Nails, was almost two years ago. I only got manicures and pedicures so I only came monthly sometimes more. I was not one of those females that had to be in the nail salon weekly. I let my natural beauty work for itself.

We made small talk as she worked hard on my nails filing and buffing them.

"How's everything been, girl?" She asked. She was a very stylish female. She could have shown that thing behind us how to dress.

"I've been good. Jelly is working and everything. Work has been ok. So I guess you could say good."

She smiled. "That's what I like to hear. I'm glad yall doing ok. Girl, you won't believe it but I had action in here last week. I got into a fight in the damn shop. Su Li wanted to fire me and everything."

I sipped my sparkling water and busted out laughing. Who the hell gets into a fight in the nail shop?

"Girl you are crazy."

"I'm serious. It's nothing, though. Su Li know she can't fire me because I bring all the clientele in here and she knows there is nobody fucking with me on the nails. I'm leaving in a month anyway on the first. My building will be ready."

"Well, that's a blessing hard work certainly pays off. I'm laughing at you but why Jonelle's crazy ass tried to come for me when I was watching her daughter."

"You say that you are drama free but you got more drama than me. I see you must have finally gave in with Zayvion."

"Nope. Girl you know I love Jelly. I would never disrespect our relationship like that. The thought has crossed my mind."

"You're better than me. Hell, I would not have spoken to that wench Jackie if I were you. Look at her over there thinking she is Petersburg's next top model."

We were chatting away and she was almost done with my nails. I got a simple design.

I paid her and thanked her for hooking me up as usual.

Now that my nails were taken care of I could go out and get a little shopping done. For some reason, I felt good after talking with Paris. Maybe I would call her sometimes and we could hang out. Maybe I needed a friend to talk to.

Once I got to the mall I went to the stores I always frequented and got the usual stuff, smell good lotions and candles, I got some underwear and a few pairs of jeans, and some shoes for Jelly. He loved to dress so he would love the shoes. I would always buy him gifts, that was just what I did. I didn't want to carry too many bags so I decided to cut the trip short.

I passed by Justice, girls store and I saw a cute dress on display that would look pretty on Niya. I was about to go in the store but I stopped in my tracks. Jacquee was in the nail salon getting nails her and lashes done so there was no reason that she couldn't buy her own child a dress. The services she got where not cheap so I know she could afford a dress. As much as I loved Jelly I was slowly but surely cutting back on doing everything for him and his kids. I never told him this directly but he should have known.

People were going to stop thinking that they could ass over me.

After hearing Paris say she was leaving and getting her own salon I wondered could I do the same thing. Leave my job and start anew with my own business. I was definitely going to look into it. I had all these great ideas and was feeling invincible.

Then I heard her before I saw here.

Jonelle husky voice ass was walking through the food court holding on to some light bright fine guy. She was laughing as she walked closely holding his hands. He must have said something really funny because she was all smiles and giggles. I had never seen her look this way. I didn't know the bougie chick mouth could form into a genuine smile. She quickly wiped the smile off her face. It was my time to beam.

Yeah, buddy. She was caught. I smiled back at her and winked. I had her where I wanted her. Now that I knew I ruffled her feathers, I kept on going. Her secret was safe with me for now. I had all the ammunition I needed to make her suffer. With a mile-wide smile on my face, I got in my car.

Jonelle ass was off the chain. She did all this carrying on

about her man and she was out here with that d boy. He was a switch from Zayvion. I mean he was fine and everything but he was not the type of guy I would have went for. If me and Jelly ever ended a street nigga couldn't even look at me. I wanted children and a family and I did not want to get involved with anyone who was headed in the direction of jail or the graveyard. That's why I stayed on Jelly so hard.

So many times I toyed with the idea of saying something to Zayvion but I respected his relationship and mine, although our significant others didn't. This shit was crazy. Tucking thoughts of Jonelle's messy ass and her fine man in the back of my mind I was almost home. My thoughts were now to get home to cook Jelly dinner and have it ready for him or to take him out.

When I got in the house I thought my eyes were deceiving me. The tv was missing, the PS4 and all the games and movies were gone. I dropped all my shopping bags on the floor and begin to run through the house to see what else was missing. Someone had robbed us. I ran back in the living room to grab my phone out of my bag to call Jelly.

The phone just kept ringing.

"Dammit pick up the phone Jelly."

I knew that he was off by now so why wasn't he answering. I sat on the bed. I was about to call the police when I noticed the open closet doors.

All of Jelly's stuff was gone. The only thing left were some old beat up New Balances that he would wear to work.

I dropped the phone in confusion. What the hell was going on?

No this sorry sack of dog shit did not move out on me while I was at work. This fool had me thinking that we were back going strong and he had moved out. The coward could have at least said he was leaving. I would be lying if I said I was not hurt. This was some low down mess here.

I begin to have all kinds of thoughts. This is probably why that old hag Jacquee was smiling in my face earlier. I wonder does she have anything to do with this? She has been wanting Jelly back ever since forever.

I needed some answers. I called his number and it went straight to voicemail. He already knew what time it was when I called him a few minutes ago. I could not believe this shit.

I didn't know what to do so I sat in the floor Indian style and cried. I guess this was the thanks I got for trying to change a grown ass man. Jelly never was going to change for me. I now realized that he took that job for his own selfish needs. He had used me to make a come up. I felt so betrayed. I wasn't too sad because he moved out but the way he went about doing things, he simply should have told me this was not what he wanted. The entire time I was sitting around having high hopes and big dreams about our future when here he was planning his future without me.

What would people think about me or say about me? This had to be some embarrassing mess. I prided myself on my happy relationship. I needed to talk to Jelly to see what he had to say so I tried to call him again.

I cried so much that I now had snot running down my nose. The tears would not stop falling. I was going to be alone. I did not want to be by myself.

After blowing my nose and wiping my face I called Jelly. I was about to hang up when he answered.

"Hello."

I never thought I would miss hearing the sound of his voice.

"Jelly. How could you just leave me like this?" My voice cracked.

I could hear laughter in the background. Then I heard a scuffle as if someone were fighting. Then I heard Jacquee's voice.

All my tears subsided. He had left me for her. I was so upset that I wanted to hang the phone up and beat the hell out of them both.

"So you thought you were going to live happily ever after with my man huh? Thanks for paying his child support and doing so well by my kids these last four years. You have got to be the dumbest woman on earth."

I didn't have anything to say. I just listened to her talk.

"Don't call Jelly anymore because he is my man and he is going to be a father to his three kids. Do you understand me?"

Wait. They don't have three children they only have two that means that she was pregnant. She did look a little thick in the middle earlier. My temperature began to rise.

She was still trying to talk on the other end when I heard Jelly yell, "Give me my fucking phone," before the call disconnected.

After that phone call, I knew that I had to move on with my life and that I had been forcing myself into an unhealthy relationship. I just wanted to be loved but I knew that in due time I would find it. To take my mind off Jelly I cleaned up and went through the house and got rid of all my reminders of him.

On my way to the garbage can I spotted Jonelle. The way I felt I would spare her a beat down if she didn't say anything out of the way. Of course, she thought she was a bad ass so she tried it.

"Congratulations Amika," she smirked.

She wasn't taking out any garbage, she only came near me to start some shit with me.

"Take that phony act somewhere else. I don't need your congratulations. I don't need you saying a word to me."

I spit my words at her like poisonous venom.

"I'm shocked Jelly married you. Well now you can stop looking at my man." She sneered.

"I'm not married to anybody!"

I looked at with squinted eyes. What the hell was she talking about? Jonelle burst out laughing.

"Oops. They did say he married Jacquee. Ain't nobody marrying your lame ass. I might invite you to my wedding or let you come and watch all the kids during the ceremony." She twirled her big engagement ring around on her finger. It should have been a symbol of love and something beautiful, her snake ass didn't deserve that man or the ring. Here I was going crazy trying to make a man love me and she had a good man who loved her unconditionally. Love was not on time for me and it was about to be cut off for her as well. I faced Jonelle and looked up at the tall giraffe. The look on my face meant I was serious.

"You keep messing with me, there will be no wedding for you boo."

With that being said I walked off like a boss, turning giving her my ass to kiss.

CHAPTER 7 ZAYVION

It is never good to lie to your significant other. If you tell one lie you have to tell another one, and then another one. It's a snowball effect. I was now beginning to look at Jonelle in an entire different light. She had lied to me and it was all catching up to her. I didn't know who this woman was I was engaged to. Luckily, I was taking the blinders off and could see things for what they really were.

Jonelle never quite told me what she got arrested for, even after I took my money to get her out. I had to find it out in court that she got arrested for speeding and a suspended license and that this was not her first offense.

"Jonelle Lynn how and why is your license suspended?"

"I don't know Zay could be a misunderstanding or mistake. I will look into it."

Well baby mama kept giving me the run around so I looked her charges up online. Public records were free. I didn't want to go behind her back but at the same time I didn't want to be getting caught up in no mess. I worked entirely too hard to lose everything. When I was younger I called myself hustling or getting money but I knew that it was nothing long term. I used that money to help me get my stuff together. Jonelle wanted it to be a long-term career move. Unless I was going to own a damn cartel, I did not see a future with me in the drug game.

Jonelle didn't say it to me but I know that she was not happy with me just being a working man. I tried to make her happy and go above and beyond but it seems my best was never enough for her.

She showed me the house that she wanted and I worked my ass off to get it but what was going to be the point if she was never going to be around. All she wanted to do was party. When was she going to grow up? I never imagined I would be here reevaluating my relationship but this shit had gotten out of hand.

I was very serious about my relationships. What me and

Jonelle had was slowly falling apart but I was getting closer to God. It was more to life than what I was dealing with so I filled the void with church and things seemed to be going in a positive direction since I made the decision to get back into church.

When Sunday came I got Joy up and ready while Jonelle laid in bed snoring getting the best sleep of her life. She should have got up and came with us but that was not happening I was not going to bother asking her. She never attended service with us. I made us both a bowl of oatmeal and toast and we ate together after blessing our meal. I said it once and I'll say it again, Joy was not going to grow up to be anything like her mother. I was making sure of that.

We left without disturbing Jonelle. She wanted to sleep so that's where we left her.

When we got to church we took our seats where we would regularly sit. Jonelle's mother was up in the choir stand singing. She made eye contact with us as we sat down. I'm sure she was wondering where her daughter was. The praise and worship service seemed to go by fast. The message was one that was right on time. I think that the preacher must have known my heart as he spoke from Isaiah 43,16-21, about a new beginning.

With fervor in his voice he spoke in a strong black jeremiad, "Life is full of ends but every end is a new beginning, and we are continually coming to the point where we close one chapter, but we always can turn and open a new and better and a diviner chapter."

He looked directly at me, then pulled out his handkerchief. The choir was behind him singing the praise. Shouts to glory could be heard in the congregation. There were people standing and shouting "Amen" and "Hallelujah". I looked over at my daughter and Joy sat beside me listening attentively.

Looking ahead and listening to the word, the pastor brought me to my feet when he said, "New beginnings with God take more effort, but God says in many ways, "I would like to do new things with you." When I say I needed this confirmation and word, I really needed it.

I had been holding on to a relationship that was not going anywhere. I loved Jonelle but I was not in love with her. There was no reason that I should marry a woman that I was not in love with. As if that was not enough she did not have the same love for the Lord or her own child as I did. It was time for me to move on. I was going to call the engagement off.

I know my grandmother who raised me, God rest her soul, she used to always tell me "love isn't always on time." Now I knew what that meant. I had been putting forth all this effort for a woman who did not love me but she loved me for what I could do. She was so selfish that she was willing to lie and be dishonest just to get what she wanted. Well it all stopped now.

After church, I went to Golden Corral to get rolls for dinner, while Joy went with her grandmother. Cherry had invited us back for Sunday dinner. Normally we would go there for a big meal after service. Today was no different. While I was waiting for the orders of rolls my coworker Hazel, an older woman, came to sit beside me. She was related to Amika, I think it was her aunt, she had the same light skin, freckles and red hair color. She too had come from the same church I had just left from. Neenah came in and looked at us.

"Hmph. I thought Jonelle was shitting me when she said you

were messing with Amika. You terrible Zayvion."

Hazel looked at her like she was crazy. She was not paying Neenah any attention. "I'll see you at work Zayvion," before she excused herself. She was not going to entertain that fool.

Neenah was low key salty because I turned her down every chance she got.

"Mind your business sometimes Neenah." I was not going to feed into her mess.

"You're going to wish that you minded yours a little more."

I looked at her puzzled.

The server came up to me with the three boxes of hot dinner rolls.

Neenah looked around I guess she was waiting on someone. The over seductive cashier from Walmart, Moni approached her. It was definitely my time to go. She came up with a big toothy grin exposing her gold teeth. Hood's finest.

I was not going straight to hell after church for sitting here messing with these heathens.

***

When I got to Cherry's house I parked on the street. There

were quite a few family and church family at the house. Jonelle pulled up behind me. Her tinted window was down but she had someone in the car, as she left it running. I was surprised to even see her there but she was just the person I wanted to see. She followed me into the house into the kitchen. All the other guests were in the den and in the back deck. The only person in the kitchen was Cherry and she was taking the food out of the oven.

Jonelle spoke to me all dry like she barely wanted to part her lips.

"Jonelle, why would you speak to your future husband like that?"

Little did she know there was no future in me being her husband. I figured now was a good time as ever to say it. If not now, when?

"It's ok. Cherry. There won't be a wedding. I can't marry your daughter."

Her mouth fell open.

"What the hell is going on with yall? Jonelle what did you do?"

She stood by the door and tried to feign innocence.

I spoke again, "It's no point in beating around the bush. We have not been happy for some time now. Your daughter wants a thug in her life. I was not street enough for her. Tell her Jonelle. Tell your mother how you got a thing for hood niggas."

Jonelle looked stupid in the face. I don't think she wanted her mother to know she was not an angel like she carried on to be.

"Shut the fuck up, Zay!"

"You are not going to stand in my house on a Sunday and talk like this Jonelle Lynn Todd. I'm sorry that I made you this way. Maybe I gave you too much and this was the repayment I got for trying to be a good mother. I have an undercover thot for a daughter that does not give five cents about her child."

Jonelle started crying. Her mother was the only person that could put her in her place.

We heard a car horn beeping.

"Well I'm sorry I couldn't be the wife and mother yall wanted me to be. I'm really sorry."

She took off her ring and threw it in my direction and ran to the door. There was some man in the car waiting in the driver's seat.

"Come back here Jonelle!"

Cherry screamed for her only child to come back but the guy driving the car pulled off in a hurry as soon as she put her foot in the car.

I wanted new beginnings and she had hers already. I was no longer hungry. My mood was all messed up. Jonelle was so self-centered she didn't speak to her child or bother taking her with her. Well I was not allowing my daughter to go with her anyway. We were truly over.

CHAPTER 8 JONELLE

The heart wants what the heart wants. I woke up realizing that I was not about to keep playing around. Monster was who I wanted to be with. There was no man or child that was going to stop me from being happy. When Monster called me I got rolled out of bed. He demanded my attention and I jumped up to cater to him. He had me doing things that I never did before. Using some of the money I had saved up I got an apartment. That's where we would spend most of our time. I was dividing my time between being there and at home with Zayvion and Joy. I was tired of living a double life. Monster wanted me to leave Zayvion. He told me I could bring Joy with me but I never wanted her in the first place so she was fine right where she was.

Snuggled up close to Monster, I didn't want him to leave my side. I never cared if Zay was coming or going. I needed to be with Monster though. I had my legs wrapped around him so he couldn't get up.

We were watching a movie. I loved to spend quality time with him just chilling. I had made hot wings for us to snack on and I had him some cold beer. I watched him closely as he smoked. Since I found out that I was pregnant I was no longer indulging in smoking. All the partying and fun things we used to do in the beginning had stopped now. I was being the wife to Monster that I never was to Zay. I really try hard not to compare the two but it was hard.

Monster's phone rang. "Move back Jonelle. I need to take this call."

"Dang I was just getting comfortable. Do I have to move?"

He lifted my leg and stood up.

Monster was fine as ever. He had on some light blue distressed Robin's jeans and a white t-shirt showing off his tattooed arms. His bald head was shaved and his beard was on point zaddy was looking good. Whoever he was talking to I hope he didn't take too long to talk to them I needed all of his attention.

In a year me and him had been through some things so I felt like he had no choice but to be with me. When I got arrested I was speeding because I had just dropped off his packages. I was rushing trying to get back to my baby.

Living in the fast lane I messed around and let my license get suspended for unpaid tickets. These were tickets that I had got when I had my old car. Nobody told me that the tickets followed you when you got a new car and didn't pay them. I didn't know. I had never even made a car payment or insurance payment. I was used to Zay handling all of that. So when the blue lights came on and I got pulled that day, I was going way above the speed limit with a suspended license. This was not my first time being made aware of the license situation nor was it my first time going to jail. I just managed to hide it from Zayvion very well.

I didn't like hiding things from him because all in all he was good to me but it was what it was. If I had it my way I never would have called him to get me out but Neenah wouldn't come and get me. I had put some distance from her too because she was supposed to be my closest friend and now she was my biggest hater. Ever since she found out that me and Monster was official she was salty.

"Jonelle how you going just fuck with my family. You got a good man and you going throw it all away like that for Monster? What's wrong with you?"

I can't believe she really came out of her mouth and said that. I thought she would be happy for me but she wasn't.

Then the other biggest hater Moni tried to throw shit in the game every chance she got. She wanted Monster really bad. She might have got him if I didn't want him. Hell she wanted any man. I had heard about her trying to holla at Zayvion as well. I was ready to fight her too. I was just out here in the streets living it up carefree.

I was never cool with Moni like that in the first place because her low budget ass wanted to be me but I cut Neenah off, especially after she didn't come get me from jail. She sent me straight to voicemail. All the dirt I had done with her and she didn't even have my back the one time I needed her to. I got over it though it was cool. I would be ok with her as a friend too. She never meant me any good.

I went by my mother's house one day to see Joy. I guess because it was almost time for my baby to be born I wanted to see my little girl. Her birthday was approaching and I kind of missed her. She was living with Zayvion. They moved out of the loft and into the home that I was supposed to have been in. The home that I had picked out everything for. At least they were happy.

Waddling out of the car I went in the house. I was due any day now. I guess today was the day that my son was going to come into the world as my water broke soon as I walked in the living room. Cherry rushed me to the hospital and she called Zay there to meet her there to get Joy. While experiencing some of the worse pain ever, I asked her to call Monster. She did but was not picking up. He knew that I was due any day now. What could be more important to him than the birth of his firstborn? I wanted to wait until he was there but that was not going to happen.

I was going to have his son without him. The pain was

unbearable. I was ready to deliver! Just take the pain from me. Mama had the car on two wheels getting us to the hospital, when we arrived the birthing staff was waiting for me.

"Mama please try to call Monster again please," I whimpered in pain. I couldn't do anything without him.

Zayvion arrived just in time to get Joy from my mother. Unfortunately, Joy didn't want to leave her side so she took her in the waiting room with her.

"Mama don't go. I don't want to do this by myself."

Before she could respond all I heard was, "You don't have to Jonelle. I'll be here for you."

I almost passed out hearing Zayvion's voice.

"I'll be right here waiting for you with Joy."

She kissed me and left out of the room.

My contractions were so close that I was not able to get the epidural that was scheduled to have. I was having a natural birth. This was not in my plans.

Zayvion was right on time. All the ugly mess I did to him and he was still the bigger person and stood by my side.

Where the hell was Monster?

"Aghhhhhhhhh." I writhed in pain in the bed. I felt the strongest, most severe pain, like am amplified charlie horse as my baby was on the way out of the birth canal. The doctor had my legs in the air in the stirrups.

Zayvion was holding my hand and wiping my forehead, "Breathe Jonelle. Relax and take a deep breath."

My mouth was dry as the desert. Zay was so attentive that he fed me ice chips. It cracked a smile at him. It felt like he was the one that belonged here with me in the first place. A sharp pain shot through me, turning my smile into an ugly frown. I could feel it from the top of my stomach to the bottom of my yoni. And my back was on fire! The doctor yelled for me to push. I pushed down and felt like I had to have a bowel movement.

Messiah Todd slid into the world at nine pounds and three ounces. He had some lungs on him. Taking his first breaths on his own, just like he was crying so was I. I was crying tears of joy and relief. Glad to have this big baby out of me. I could finally breathe myself now. I was tired and spent, all I wanted to do was rest. Zayvion had come in and took charge. He even cut the cord.

Standing to the side it almost looked like he was crying. I understand he was there for me, but what the hell did he have a reason to shed tears for?

After the nurses cleaned him up they placed the baby in my arms. Swaddled in a blue blanket I could see exactly why Zayvion had gotten emotional. The baby was an exact replica of him. It was always something.

CHAPTER 9 AMIKA

Now that I had gotten rid of all the things weighing me down I felt free. I thought I was not going to be able to make it without a man. Not just Jelly but a man period. Let me tell you a little about myself. I always kept a man around. Ever since I was old enough to deal with the opposite sex I thought a woman was supposed to have a man. I used to read a lot of romance novels so I believed that men and women got together and lived happily ever. Well what a lie.

I fought so hard for my relationship for Jelly because I wanted to be in a relationship so bad. It did not matter to me that it was a one sided relationship. I just wanted to be coupled with somebody. My thought process was that it made you more of a woman if you had a man by your side.

Since Jelly left I started back going to church. Zay invited me with him and Joy. My aunt Hazel had been trying for the longest to get me back in the house of the Lord. Once me and Zayvion both found ourselves single we started spending a lot of time together. I hoped that we would actually grow into something more but we never did. I won't lie and say that I was not attracted to him. He was still fine as ever. He was the first man that valued my friendship and didn't want to cross the line. I could respect that.

I was sad to see him and Joy move away once their house was built. I had gotten used to spending time with them. Since the move I had not been in daily contact with Zayvion. Maybe it was for the better so I wouldn't get all in my feelings.

Tired of working for Lauryn I went to work one morning and handed her my letter of resignation before class started and the children arrived. I was taking charge of my life in every department.

"What is this Amika?"

"It's my resignation letter. I quit effective immediately."

She stood there with her mouth wide open. "You can't do that."

"The hell if I can't. Watch me."

I cleared out my desk and grabbed my few items and left. Thanks to Zayvion pushing me I decided to open a small at home childcare center. I too was going to be moving out of the lofts soon. I was ready for my new beginnings. I was motivated and excited after Zay kept talking about "new beginnings", and how it was time for a positive change. Leaving my job was one of the best decisions I could have made.

One day while I was out pumping gas Jelly pulled up beside me driving an old black Taurus. My first instinct was to stick my middle finger up at him. He whipped the car in a circle pulling right behind me. The hooptie must have needed to be refueled.

"You can't speak Amika? Damn it's like that, lil nigga?"

He smiled showing a mouth full of gold teeth, with grills. As usual he was dressed fresh to death. I was just about to say he made a come up but that car he drove told another story

In a sing song voice I said, "Hey, Jelly."

"I see you looking good. That booty still fat and you still looking right."

I laughed. He was still clowning I see.

"Thanks. You look aight yourself."

When he left me high and dry, moving out skipping out on me and the bills I said that when I saw him on sight I was going to spit in his face or some other shit but I was trying to get myself together so I forgave him. I would never forget how he used me and left me but I forgave him. I accepted the fact that he could not do anything to me that I didn't allow. The way he treated me I was at fault for putting up with it. At any point I could have put a stop to it.

"I heard about your daycare Amika. That's whats up. You finally opened your own spot. That's dope. I'm proud of you."

"Thanks. You probably were asking about me."

"You would like to know wouldn't you."

I looked at his hand. I didn't see a ring.

"So how's married life treating you?"

"Life is treating me well. Marriage not so good."

"Stop playing."

"Hold on let me go pay for this gas."

I stood by my car waiting on him to go make his purchase.

It was getting a little warm standing outside talking by a damn gas pump.

"I'm hungry. Let's go do lunch and catch up."

After he paid for his gas he followed me to Rinky Dink to get something to eat. Over lunch he told me how Jacquee carried the shit out of him. He left me to be with her and she was using him the whole time. The baby that she had was not his but it was, Jonelle's boo, Monster, it was his baby. This was too much. I sipped my lemonade to this crazy story.

He tried to do me dirty and his ass got served. Karma had come around heavy on Jelly and Jonelle. Monster ended up leaving her to be with Jacquee. They moved to North Carolina. Being the woman that she was, with her four other children being older she took them and the newborn with her but she left Jelly's son and daughter with him. What was it with these women leaving their kids behind? They act like they were getting a whole new slate to start fresh. Never in a million years would I have left my own flesh and blood behind to be with a man. What kind of love was that?

It was good seeing Jelly and catching up with him. We

exchanged numbers. Meanwhile I was also pursuing my painting and had got some of my art in the Ward Center. After I won second place in the art contest I was all in. Something so simple and relaxing was proving to be so much more. Life was good. I was finally happy.

As I said me and Jelly exchanged numbers and started back talking. We went on a few dates and we were taking things one day at a time. He truly was a changed person now and was stepping up to the plate. He was not doing it for me he was doing it for himself and his two children. I was very proud of him.

If I could stick with him when he was not doing shit with his life now that he was getting it right, I was definitely going to be there for him.

During our time apart I learned to love myself and put myself first so now I was able to open my heart to someone else. Life had a funny way of working things out. I had finally fell in love and this time it was real. We had been through all of this and love was right here in front of us the entire time. Me and Jelly closed our chapter in the past and started a beautiful new beginning.

CHAPTER 10 ZAYVION

As a proud father of a son and a daughter it was only right that I get married to Jonelle. We were married before she left the hospital. I made the mistake once of letting her slip away well it was not going to be so easy this time. Maybe had I spent just a little more time at home with her she never would have to went the route that she did. I really wanted to be with her so we were going to get through our issues.

I had to make Jonelle understand that there was no running away from problems. She liked to run from her problems. Once again had I been around more maybe the lines of communication never would have been crossed. Now that I had my girl back I was not going to lose her. I had already forgiven her that's why I had no problem with being there during the delivery.

She never told me that she was pregnant by me but I knew

that it was my child the moment her mother told me she was pregnant. Had I not shown up with her I was still going to be in my son's life just as well as my daughter.

Jonelle was a completely changed person. She cut off all of her so called friends and she started going to church with us. I was even able to get her to apologize to Amika. I wanted her to know that we were just friends it was never anything between us. There could have been but I never made a move because I didn't want to ruin a friendship.

Jonelle had went back to school to be a nurse. We decided that she should do something other than be a stay at home mother. This gave her a sense of fulfillment and purpose. I was happy that she created her own identity other than just being a wife and mother. Everything worked out just the way it was supposed to.

Throughout everything we went through I learned a valuable lesson. We all mess up that's just what humans do. We've all said some ugly hurtful things we later wish we could take back. We do things we wish we could take back as well. We miss opportunities, waiting and seeking others, which are not guaranteed. This happens in all parts of our lives, from relationships to friendships. Sometimes we make mistakes, but you have to forgive and forget. This has been a lesson and a blessing to me. Sometimes we hurt the people we love, sometimes we disappoint God.

For all these reasons, I decided to change my life and open my heart to Jonelle. I could not do it alone. I needed her with me. There is no other woman that I would rather go through my trials and tribulations with. We had been through too much in just a short time. She was just right for me.

Because we all mess up, we like to start over—to turn our backs on the past. I was ready for my new beginnings. Looking forward to our bright future, hoping that this time around, things are going to be much better. I know that in my heart they will be this time. There's something exciting about starting over—new challenges, new experiences, new opportunities. I wanted it all and I wanted it with Jonelle. I know now that the future holds the hope for something better and love isn't always on time.

AUTHORS NOTE

If you have enjoyed this book, please consider writing a review on Amazon. It really does make a difference. Thanks for your support. If you are interested in updates from me, please sign up for my newsletter and mailing list, The Forbes List at TiffanyForbes.com

Thanks,

Author Tiffany Forbes ♥☐

MEET THE AUTHOR

Author Tiffany Forbes 4/30/16
@Urban Moon Books, Chesapeake VA

https://www.facebook.com/AuthorTiffanyF/
https://www.instagram.com/authortiffanyf
https://twitter.com/AuthorTiffanyF

More Books By Author Tiffany Forbes

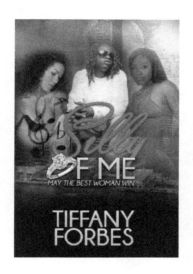

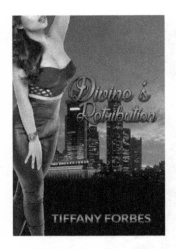

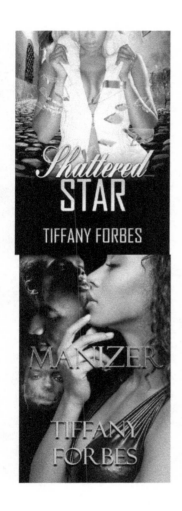

CPSIA information can be obtained
at www.ICGtesting.com
Printed in the USA
LVHW111726090320
649444LV00004B/863